# A WRONG NOTE

Frank, Chet, and Joe all got up to help, and for the next twenty minutes, they played a really serious game of musical chairs. Frank forgot all about Dylan and Crush as he ran for a seat, often ending up with his bottom landing hard on the grass when one of his classmates beat him to it. The kids were getting all sweaty, and Paul's mom frowned as she applied a bandage to one girl's elbow after she skinned it falling off a chair. "Maybe we should play—" Mrs. McMahon began.

But she never got to finish her sentence, because a yell from the makeshift stage surprised them all.

*"What happene* [illegible] his hands on his hea[illegible] ny guitar!"

CATCH UP ON ALL THE HARDY BOYS® SECRET FILES

#1 Trouble at the Arcade

#2 The Missing Mitt

#3 Mystery Map

#4 Hopping Mad

#5 A Monster of a Mystery

#6 The Bicycle Thief

#7 The Disappearing Dog

#8 Sports Sabotage

#9 The Great Coaster Caper

#10 A Rockin' Mystery

# THE HARDY BOYS®

## SECRET FILES #10

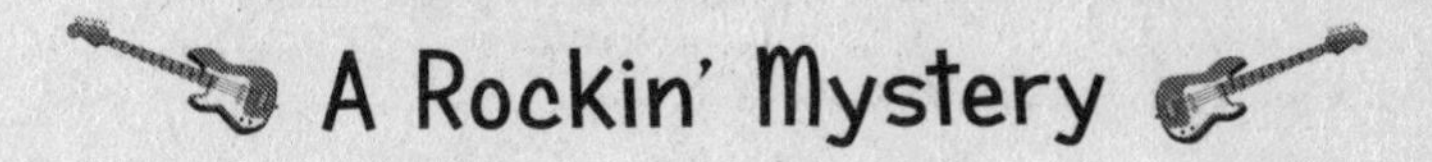

## A Rockin' Mystery

BY FRANKLIN W. DIXON

ILLUSTRATED BY SCOTT BURROUGHS

ALADDIN • NEW YORK LONDON TORONTO SYDNEY NEW DELHI

ALADDIN
An imprint of Simon & Schuster Children's Publishing Division
1230 Avenue of the Americas, New York, NY 10020
First Aladdin paperback edition October 2012

For information about special discounts for bulk purchases, please contact Simon & Schuster Special Sales at 1-866-506-1949 or business@simonandschuster.com.
The Simon & Schuster Speakers Bureau can bring authors to your live event. For more information or to book an event contact the Simon & Schuster Speakers Bureau at 1-866-248-3049 or visit our website at www.simonspeakers.com.
Designed by Lisa Vega
The text of this book was set in Garamond.
Manufactured in the United States of America 0912 OFF
10 9 8 7 6 5 4 3 2 1
Library of Congress Control Number 2012943882
ISBN 978-1-4424-1671-0
ISBN 978-1-4424-1672-7 (eBook)

# CONTENTS

# 1

# A Sour Note

"You look like a monkey, and you smell like one too!"

Nine-year-old Frank Hardy looked at his brother, Joe, and laughed as their friend Paul McMahon blew out the candles on his huge birthday cake, which was decorated to look like a dinosaur. Everyone cheered as Paul blew out all ten candles on the first try.

"Time for presents!" Paul cried as his mother started cutting up the cake. He ran over to the circle of chairs his parents had set up in his backyard and took a seat.

Joe smiled and nudged Frank. "Looks like we'd better get over there," he said. "Paul's already torn into his first gift!"

Frank laughed and shook his head. His classmate Paul seemed to be having a great time at his birthday party. They'd already played Pin the Tail on the Donkey and Red Rover, and Paul had won both. Now he was beaming as he pulled the last piece of gift wrap off Joyride, a hot new video game that had just been released days ago. It was a perfect way to spend a Saturday afternoon!

"Oh, wow!" Paul shouted, waving the game above his head. "You guys! This is great! I can't wait to play this! Thanks, Mom and Dad!"

Frank and Joe took their seats as Paul's mom came over to hand her son a piece of cake and give him a kiss. She handed cake to the kids on either

side of Paul, then went back to the table to get more.

"Hey, who's that?" Joe pulled on Frank's sleeve to get his attention and then pointed across the lawn to where an older boy, maybe fifteen or sixteen, was dragging some big pieces of equipment onto a raised platform. As they watched, three more boys came out of the house, each carrying an instrument and some more equipment.

"That's Paul's older brother, Dylan," the boys' friend Chet piped up as he took a piece of cake from Paul's mom and sat down in the chair beside Frank.

"What's he doing?" Frank asked. The older boys were scrambling around, plugging their instruments into extension cords and playing a few notes.

"He's setting up," Chet replied, digging into his cake. A dab of chocolate frosting stuck to his nose. "You guys know he's a member of Crush, right?"

"Crush?" Joe asked. "What's that?"

Chet set his fork down and stared wide-eyed

at Joe, as if Joe had just asked who Batman was. "What's *Crush*?" he asked. "You guys? It's only the best rock band in Bayport, or maybe the entire state!"

Frank shrugged. "Never heard of them."

But Joe looked thoughtful.

"Oh, riiiiight," he said. "They sing that song about pigeons?"

"'Coo-Coo-Cool My Heart,'" Chet said, nodding. "They're the best! And we're really lucky, because they're going to perform for Paul's party. Right here. Right now. *Tonight*."

"Oh, wow!" Paul shouted, a little louder than before. "A chemistry set! You guys, this is awesome! You guys?"

But the party guests were staring across the lawn now, watching the members of Crush tune up their instruments.

"He's the *coolest*," Frank heard one of the girls say as Dylan adjusted the microphone. "You know they're going to blow the competition away at the Bayport Battle of the Bands next Friday."

Frank turned around to face the girl. "What's that?"

The girl, who had curly red hair and a few freckles, widened her eyes. "You haven't heard about the Battle of the Bands?" she asked. "It's only about the most important music competition ever!"

Frank caught Joe's eye. *Hmmm.* "And you think Crush is going to win it?" Frank asked.

The girl nodded. "*Everyone* thinks Crush is going to win it," she said. "They're the best band in Bayport. Maybe in the whole state! Right, Paul?"

Paul looked up from his latest gift—a set of

colored pencils—and frowned. "I guess," he said, looking down at all his presents. "Hey, who wants to try out my new tetherball set?"

But Paul's mom swept in before anyone could respond, picking up the loose gift wrap and putting it in a garbage bag. "Okay, kids, that was the last present," she announced. "Playing a game is a good idea, Paul, but I think the tetherball game would take too long to set up. Let's all get together for a game of musical chairs while the band gets ready to play. Can you all help me arrange the chairs in a row?"

Frank, Chet, and Joe all got up to help, and for the next twenty minutes, they played a really serious game of musical chairs. Frank forgot all about Dylan and Crush as he ran for a seat, often ending up with his bottom landing hard on the grass when one of his classmates beat him to it. Paul was doing really well at first, but then Chet beat him by a second or two, and Paul was out. He stomped off, pouting. The kids were getting all sweaty, and Paul's mom frowned as she applied a bandage to one girl's elbow after she skinned it falling off a chair. "Maybe we should play—" Mrs. McMahon began.

But she never got to finish her sentence, because a yell from the makeshift stage surprised them all.

*"What happened to Lucy?"* Dylan shouted, his hands on his head. "I can't play without my guitar!"

# 2

# Gone!

"It was right here!" Dylan went on. "Someone stole my bass guitar, Lucy!"

Everyone started talking at once. Joe, who was sitting on the sidelines of the musical chairs game with the rest of the kids who had not been able to get a seat, stood up and caught Frank's eye. He raised an eyebrow. Was Lucy lost, or was she . . .

"Someone stole her!" Dylan cried, putting his head in his hands.

Chet, who'd managed to get a seat during the

last round, stood up. "Frank and Joe can help!" he yelled, pointing at the Hardy boys. "They solve mysteries, you know."

Frank's cheeks blazed a bright red. Joe knew his brother hated to be the center of attention. But personally, Joe kind of liked it.

"Sure, we can help," he said, getting to his feet. "I mean, if you guys need us. . . ."

But the band members didn't seem to be listening to him. They were gathered in a circle, talking heatedly as Dylan shook his head and shrugged.

Chet grabbed Frank by the arm and walked over to Joe. "Come on, you guys," he said, confidently leading them over to the stage. "You'll get to the bottom of this!"

The older boys barely seemed to notice as Chet, Joe, and Frank walked up.

"I only left her for a second!" Dylan was saying, clearly upset. "She was out here when we all went inside to go over the set list, and now she's gone!"

One of the other band members, a redhead with a funky mustache, crossed his arms across his chest. "You don't seriously think one of these kids took it?" he asked. "What would they want with a bass guitar?"

Chet cleared his throat loudly. "Ahem," he said, inserting himself into the middle of the group. *"Ahem."*

The redhead looked down. "Can I help you, kid?"

Chet smiled. "I hope so. May I introduce Frank and Joe Hardy?" He pointed to Joe and his brother.

Four blank faces stared down at the boys.

"Um, hello," said the drummer, who had a blond crew cut and big black glasses.

"They solve mysteries," said Chet.

The redhead rolled his eyes. "Oh, brother."

"They *are* brothers," said Chet helpfully.

The drummer scoffed. "Look, kid, I appreciate it, but I don't think your little friends are going to help us find a five-hundred-dollar bass guitar."

But Dylan held up his hand. "Hold on, Bryce," he said, looking down at the boys. "You solve mysteries?" he asked. "Like mini-detectives?"

Joe didn't like "mini." "We help out our friends," he said. "We ask questions and we figure things out. We could help you, if you like."

The other boys looked doubtful, but Dylan was nodding. "You figure things out. I like that. Yeah, I could really use your help. What do you need to know?"

Frank stepped forward. "Tell us exactly what happened," he said.

Dylan explained that the band had set up their instruments on the stage, then gone inside to work out their set list, a list of which songs they would sing and in what order. They were inside for just a few minutes, but when they came back, the bass guitar was gone.

"I need Lucy to play," Dylan said, his eyes wide. "I can't play another bass—it's not the same. And we have the Bayport Battle of the Bands coming up. If I don't get Lucy back, we'll have to forfeit!"

Joe looked at his brother. "Can you tell us more about the Bayport Battle of the Bands?" he asked.

Chet jumped in. "It's a contest. Five local bands play, and one wins. They get a cash prize and a weekly gig playing at the Keen Beans coffee shop. Crush was totally going to win!"

Dylan smiled down at Chet. "Thanks, little dude."

Chet shrugged. "It's just the truth. You guys rock!"

Paul's mom walked up to the group, looking

worried. "I searched all over the house," she told Dylan. "I didn't see Lucy anywhere."

"I told you, Mom," Dylan said. "I'm sure I left her out here."

Paul's mom bit her lip. "I just don't understand, then," she said with a sigh. "Who would have taken it . . . ?" she said, trailing off.

Joe spoke up. "Mrs. McMahon," he said, "maybe we should keep people from leaving until we've had a chance to talk to everyone? My brother Frank and I are going to help investigate. And if someone at the party took Lucy, it would be good to have everyone here."

Paul's mom looked down at Joe, surprised. "That's a good idea," she admitted, "but I'm afraid it's impossible. A few parents showed up while I was searching the house, and some guests told me they needed to get home. Five of Paul's friends have already left."

Dylan sighed.

"Let's search the house again, and the backyard," Joe suggested. "If we all split up and look, maybe we'll find something."

But twenty minutes later the boys, the band members, and Paul's parents gathered back at the stage, empty-handed.

"I didn't see anything," Dylan said sadly. "And nobody I talked to saw anything. It's like Lucy just disappeared without a trace."

Joe glanced at Frank. He looked just as disappointed as Dylan. Joe knew that both he and his brother had really hoped to find Lucy tonight.

Paul's father sighed. "Well, it's getting late," he said. "I think we'd better break up the party and let Paul's friends go home."

Dylan nodded sadly.

Joe touched his arm. "Listen," he said, "Frank and I will sleep on it, and tomorrow morning, we'll start asking around. I promise you we'll keep looking until we find Lucy or figure out what happened to her."

Dylan still looked upset, but he gave Joe a sad smile and held out his hand for Joe to shake. "Thanks, dude," he said. "I appreciate your help. You and your brother, you're all right."

Joe smiled. He loved helping people when they needed it. That's why he and Frank loved solving mysteries.

"All right, kids," Paul's mom announced, calling over to the remaining birthday

guests, who were clustered under a tree. "Thank you all for coming, but I think it's time for everyone to go home."

Dylan sighed. "I hope we find Lucy soon," he said, so quietly that only Joe and Frank could hear. "With her missing, there's no way I'll get any sleep!"

# 3

# The Six *W*s

"All right," Frank said, picking up a marker and pointing to the whiteboard. After a hearty breakfast of pancakes and sausage served up by their aunt Gertrude, he and Joe had climbed up to the tree house their dad had built them in their wooded backyard to go over what they knew about Lucy's disappearance. "Let's talk about the six *W*s."

The six *W*s were something their dad had taught them. Fenton Hardy was a successful private investigator who often worked with the police department. He said that the key to solving a mystery was to ask yourself six questions: Who, What, When, Where, Why, and How.

Frank wrote *Who?* at the top of the whiteboard.

"We don't know Who yet," Joe said, tapping his chin. "That's what we have to figure out. Who stole Dylan's guitar?"

"I'll just leave a question mark for now," Frank said.

Underneath, he wrote *What?*

"That's easy," said Joe. "The What is that someone stole Lucy."

Frank wrote that in. "The next is When," he said, writing the question on the board. "And I think the answer is 'During Paul's party.' Whoever did this must have taken Lucy when Dylan and his bandmates were inside."

"Right," said Joe. "So the next question is . . ."

"Where," Frank said, writing that on the board.

"It was from Paul's backyard," Joe said.

"Right." Frank nodded and wrote that too. He and his brother took in what they'd worked out so far.

Who?

What?—Stole Dylan's bass

When?—During Paul's party

Where?—From Paul's yard

Frank crossed his arms. "The only two left are Why and How," he said, writing the words on the board.

The boys were silent for a minute, thinking.

"Those are the hardest ones," Joe said finally. "Why would someone at Paul's party want to steal Dylan's guitar? And how did they do it during the party?"

Frank didn't know. It didn't make a lot of sense. Maybe one of their classmates wanted to learn to play the guitar, but Frank didn't think anyone from the party would stoop so low as to take someone else's. And besides, who would be bold enough to steal it from Dylan's own backyard?

Then he remembered something Dylan had told them. "There's that Bayport Battle of the Bands coming up," he said. "Remember?"

Joe nodded, his eyes lighting up. "And Dylan said he couldn't play without Lucy."

Frank tapped the tip of the marker, thinking this through. "If Crush can't play," he said, "that kind of opens up the field for the other bands, right?"

Joe nodded again. "It could make it easier for them to win," he reasoned. "And the prizes were pretty good, right?"

"Uh-huh," Frank said, remembering. "Some

cash and a weekly gig playing at a coffee shop."

Joe frowned. "Maybe someone from one of those other bands stole Lucy?"

Frank thought about that. "Or maybe someone working for one of those other bands," he suggested. "I think that's the only explanation that makes sense."

He and Joe looked at each other.

"How do we find out who the other bands are?" Joe asked.

Frank smiled. "That," he said, "is what the Internet is for!"

The boys rushed down the ladder to their backyard, then ran back to the house and into their dad's empty study.

"DAD!" Joe yelled. "Can we use your computer?"

"Sure!" His father's answer came from upstairs.

Frank grabbed the mouse and opened up to his father's home page. Frank typed in "Bayport Battle of the Bands" and hit the search button.

"Here we go," Frank murmured as a link to the Battle of the Bands site came up. He clicked on it, then scrolled down.

The site listed five local bands:

Crush

The Mean Willies

Babraham Lincoln

Geezers with Accordions

The Rock-a-Byes

"Any of those sound familiar?" Frank asked his brother. He knew Joe listened to the radio more than he did.

Joe shook his head. "Is there a way to get their contact information?"

Frank looked over the site. He clicked on a link labeled "For More Information," then chuckled as he scrolled down. "Check it out," he said, pointing the mouse at "Contact Person."

Joe laughed. The site listed the contact person for the Battle of the Bands as "Susie Zermeño." One of their classmates and Little League teammates on the Bayport Bandits was Cissy "Speedy" Zermeño.

"That can't be a very common last name," Joe observed. "Do you think they're related?"

"Let's find out tomorrow at baseball practice," said Frank. "Maybe Speedy can help us find Lucy!"

# 4

# A Speedy Answer

"You can do it, Joe!" Chet yelled at baseball practice the next day. Joe stood at bat, staring down Adam Ackerman, who was playing pitcher for the other team. Joe's team was down 3–1, and practice was nearly over, but the bases were loaded. He knew he had to get on base!

Adam squinted at him and let loose a curveball. Joe bit his lip, pulled back the bat, and swung to the sky. He heard a sharp *crack* and saw the ball take flight. Joe dropped the bat and took off running for first base.

Speedy Zermeño was playing second base, and Joe could see her running for the ball, then backing up to get behind it. It bounced off her glove, then fell to the ground. She scrambled for it, managed to get it into her glove, and then ran back to second base just in time to get the runner from first base out. Even worse, she reeled back and made a perfect throw to third base. Joe's stomach sank. The third baseman caught it just as the runner from second tried to slide in.

Double play. That made three outs!

"Okay, kids, let's call that a practice," the coach called, and Joe sank down to the grass. Darn that Speedy Zermeño! She was always outplaying him, and he was sick of it!

He sighed. *Be sportsmanlike,* he heard his dad saying in his head. *It's nice to win, but it's more important to be a good sport.* Joe reluctantly got to his feet and started walking back to the dugout, where his teammates were collecting their things. Speedy was walking in from second base, and she fell into step beside him after a few feet.

"That was a good hit, Joe," she said earnestly. Then she broke into a smile. "Too bad the best second baseman in the whole league was there to catch it!"

Joe groaned. *Sportsmanlike,* he reminded himself. "That was a good play, Speedy," he muttered.

"Thanks," Speedy replied, her smile widening.

"Hey, if you and your brother ever need any tips, I'd be happy to give you some private coaching."

*Sportsmanlike,* Joe thought as he plodded into the dugout. *Sportsmanlike. Sportsmanlike!*

"Hey, Joe. Hey, Speedy." Frank stepped forward to greet them. "Joe, did you ask her already?"

Joe looked blankly at his brother. "Ask her?"

"About *Susie,*" Frank reminded him.

*Oh, riiiiight.* Joe remembered now.

"Hey, Speedy," he said as she hauled her backpack onto her back, "do you know a Susie Zermeño? Is that, like, a relative of yours?"

Speedy stared at him. "A relative? Uh, that's my mom," she explained, looking over at the parking lot. "Actually, she's supposed to pick me up any minute. Why?"

Frank met Joe's eyes. "Is your mom involved with the Bayport Battle of the Bands?" he asked her.

Speedy turned back to face them. "Yeah," she

said. "My mom used to tour as a backup singer for this funk band, the Mignogna Brothers. Maybe you've heard of them?"

Joe nodded. He was pretty sure his dad had a Mignogna Brothers record. He could remember the cover, with a bearded guy on the front. "Sure."

Speedy shrugged. "Anyway, she *looooves* music. So three years ago she had the idea for a Bayport Battle of the Bands." She turned back to the parking lot, where a black SUV had just pulled in. "Hey, there she is! You guys want a ride?"

Joe looked at Frank. They'd planned to walk, but it would be great to get a chance to talk to Speedy's mom.

"That would be great," Frank said.

They walked over to the SUV, and Speedy asked her mom if she'd give the boys a ride. She happily said yes, and Speedy and the boys piled into the backseat.

"Hey, so, can I ask a question, Mrs. Zermeño?" Joe asked once they were on their way.

Mrs. Zermeño caught his eye in the rearview mirror. "Sure."

"You run the Bayport Battle of the Bands?"

Mrs. Zermeño smiled. "I sure do," she replied, making a left turn. "But I can't get you backstage, if that's what you were going to ask."

"Oh, that's not it," Joe said. He explained that Lucy had gone missing at Paul's party. Then he told her what he and Frank had talked about—that maybe someone from one of the other bands might know something.

Mrs. Zermeño looked concerned. "That's terrible," she said. "I feel just awful for Dylan; he's a nice kid and a very talented musician. But, boys, you know everyone is innocent until proven guilty, right? I'm okay with you asking the other bands some questions, but I don't want you to accuse them without knowing they did something wrong."

Frank leaned forward. "Oh, we understand, Mrs. Zermeño," he said. "Asking questions is all we do. We just want to get some information."

Mrs. Zermeño looked thoughtful. "Okay," she said finally. She'd just pulled onto the boys' street. "Is that your house?"

The brothers directed her into the driveway, and as they piled out, Mrs. Zermeño got out and opened the trunk to pull out a folder. "This car is my mobile office," she told Joe with a smile. Joe just nodded. It sounded like something his dad would say.

From the folder, Mrs. Zermeño pulled out a crisp white printout. "Here's the flyer I've been passing out," she said, handing the sheet to Joe. "It has the website and contact person for each band. Just remember what I told you, kids: innocent until proven guilty."

"Sure," Joe muttered. But he was distracted. He'd looked at the sheet and gotten a big surprise!

"Bye, kids," Mrs. Zermeño said, climbing back into the driver's seat.

Speedy waved through the window. "See you later!"

Frank and Joe waved. As soon as the SUV reached the end of the driveway, Joe grabbed his brother's arm. "Check it out!"

He held up the sheet and pointed. Under the band the Mean Willies, a familiar name was listed. Frank saw it and gasped.

*"Adam Ackerman!"*

# 5

# The Mean Willies

"Adam Ackerman can be such a bully—it wouldn't surprise me at all if he stole Lucy so his band could beat Crush!" Joe fumed to Frank as they entered the lunchroom the next day.

Frank nodded, fingering the brown-bag lunch Aunt Gertrude had packed for him. He wasn't hungry for food yet—he was hungry for justice! "Let's find him and talk to him right now," he said.

Adam sat at a table by the window with a group of his friends. As he and Joe approached, Adam and his friends started snickering and saying things like "Nerd alert," but Frank was too intent on finding Lucy to let it bother him.

"Adam," he said simply, "we need to talk to you."

The other boys kept snickering, but Adam just looked at the brothers, wiped his mouth with a napkin, and stood up. "Let's make this quick," he said. He led the boys to a quiet corner of the lunch-room and turned to face them, looking bored. "All right, what do you want?"

Frank had been imagining this moment since they'd seen Adam's name the day before, but he still didn't know where to start. Finally he spat out, "You're in a band!"

Adam looked surprised, but pleased. "That's right," he said, holding his head a little higher. "I've taken up the drums! And I started a band called the Mean Willies. We're *awesome*, for real!

We're going to mop up at the Battle of the Bands this Friday. Just you wait!"

Frank and Joe exchanged looks. Adam was suspiciously confident.

"Why are you so sure of that?" Joe asked, moving closer to Adam. "Is it because you . . . stole Crush's bass guitar?"

Adam looked confused. "What?"

"You went to Paul's party!" Frank jumped in, getting up in Adam's face. "You knew that Crush would be your biggest competitor at the Battle of the Bands! So when Crush was getting ready to play and we were all distracted playing musical chairs, you pounced!"

Adam blinked. He looked kind of upset now. "Pounced?"

"You stole Lucy!" Joe went on. "Dylan's bass guitar! Because you knew without it,

Crush couldn't play—and your stupid band would have a better chance of winning the battle!"

Now Adam looked stunned. "Stupid?!"

"But you can't get away with it," Frank said, "because we're onto you, Adam! And we're not going to leave you alone until you return that bass guitar! You hear me?"

Adam was blinking, looking from one Hardy

to the other. Actually, Frank noted, he looked a little sick. He was probably disappointed his little plan hadn't worked! But before either brother could jump in again, Adam spoke.

"Paul had a party and he didn't invite me?" he asked in a small voice.

Frank looked at Joe. *Uh-oh.*

But hadn't Adam . . . ?

Joe's eyes widened. And Frank's stomach seemed to fall into his feet as he came to a horrible realization.

Adam *hadn't* been there. He must not have been invited.

Which meant he couldn't have stolen Lucy.

And they had just accused an innocent kid.

"Um," said Joe, looking helplessly at his brother.

Frank cleared his throat. He turned back to Adam, who was watching him with glassy eyes.

"We're really sorry," he said in a small voice. "We, um, made a mistake."

Adam frowned. "I think you just accused me of stealing something."

Joe coughed. "Oh, is that Aunt Gertrude on the other side of the lunchroom? Gotta go . . ."

Frank reached out a hand to stop his brother from making a hasty exit. "We're *really* sorry," he said again. "We got carried away."

Adam narrowed his eyes. "The Mean Willies don't have to cheat," he said. "We're too good."

Frank nodded. "And we're really looking forward to seeing you perform on Friday."

Adam's expression didn't change. For what seemed like forever, he stared Frank down.

"I think that *is* Aunt Gertrude," Frank said finally. "Um, see you later."

Joe ran off, and Frank struggled to keep up with him. They finally stopped when they were on the opposite side of the lunchroom from Adam's table.

"That went pretty terribly," Frank muttered, tossing his lunch in the trash. He wasn't hungry now.

# 6

# Salty Snap Beans

"Okay," Frank said as he and Joe settled into a seat on the bus, "let's talk about what we did wrong at lunch."

Joe groaned. They felt so bad about what had happened with Adam, they'd told Chet that they didn't feel up to playing soccer after school, like they'd planned. And they hadn't talked all afternoon about what had happened with Adam. But Joe knew Frank was right: They had to talk about it so they wouldn't make the same mistake again.

"We did what Speedy's mom told us not to do," Joe said. "We accused someone when we didn't have any evidence."

Frank nodded and sighed. "And we mentioned a party to someone we weren't sure was invited," he said. "Remember, Aunt Gertrude always says that's a bad idea."

"It sure is," Joe muttered.

"So," Frank said, sitting up. "From now on, no more accusing unless we know for sure that someone did something. Okay?"

Joe nodded. "Innocent until proven guilty," he said, echoing what Speedy's mom had told them.

"Okay," said Frank, pulling out some papers from his book bag. They had information he'd gotten last night from the bands' websites. He unfolded the printouts and showed them to Joe. "Who should we try next?"

Joe was almost too worn out from their screwup

at lunch to think about it. But then he noticed another familiar name. "Hey, look," he said. "Check out the contact name for Geezers with Accordions."

Frank smiled. "Hey, it's Wilmer Mack!"

Wilmer Mack was a nice older man the boys often saw around town walking his dog, who by coincidence was also named Lucy. Joe looked up as the bus passed through the center of town. "Doesn't Wilmer live somewhere around here?" he asked as they pulled to a stop.

Frank pointed out the window. "He lives right

there, at the Golden Lanes Retirement Village," he said. "Aunt Gertrude isn't expecting us home for an hour or two. Let's get off!"

The boys got off the bus and walked into a large brick building. Inside, raucous music was coming from a large rec room opposite the security desk. Joe looked at his brother just as Wilmer came out of the room and headed down the hall.

"Wilmer!" Frank called.

Wilmer turned around and smiled. "Well, if it isn't the Hardy boys!" he said, winking at the woman working the security desk. "Hey, do you boys like music?"

"We sure do," said Joe. "In fact, we had a couple of questions for—"

"Then come with me!" Wilmer said with a big smile. "Ruby, these boys are my guests." He strode back into the rec room, gesturing for the boys to follow him. Joe looked at Frank, shrugged, and followed Wilmer.

Inside the rec room, the music was overwhelming. Listening to it felt like being in the most fun musical arcade Joe could possibly imagine. Trumpets tooted, guitars strummed, and there was a *vrum-vrum-vrum* sound that made Joe's toes want to tap like crazy! He looked up to the stage and saw an elderly woman making the *vrum-vrum-vrum* sound on a washboard. Wilmer walked up to the stage, picked up an accordion, and began to play.

Joe and Frank looked at each other. *Wow,* Frank mouthed. It was really all there was to say.

The music pulled the boys in like a magnet. Joe soon realized that he couldn't keep still while the music was playing. The band members weren't staying still either—they swayed, two-stepped, spun in circles, and jumped happily to the music. When the first song tootled to a close, Joe realized he was out of breath.

Frank started clapping loudly, and Joe followed suit.

"That was *amazing*!" Frank cried. "Wilmer, we didn't know you played in a band!"

Wilmer smiled, wiping his face with a handkerchief. His cheeks were rosy and he'd worked up a sweat. "Not just any band," he told the boys, "a *zydeco* band."

"Zydeco?" asked Joe. "What's that?"

Wilmer's eyes sparkled. "It comes from the

French phrase *'Les haricots sont pas salés,'* which means 'The snap beans aren't salted.'"

Joe had no idea what he was talking about. "What?" he asked.

Wilmer laughed. "Zydeco is a kind of Cajun folk music that's popular down South where I come from, in Louisiana," he explained. "The Cajun folks down there speak French."

Joe still wasn't sure what that had to do with beans, but he didn't care. He just wanted them to play another song. "Play something else!" he begged. "Please?"

The band agreed, but not before the lady playing the washboard showed Joe how to do it and the drummer showed Frank how to play along on the cymbals. The next song was even better than the first. It reminded Joe of being at a carnival on a summer night, with lights flashing and games beeping and the carousel playing a pipe-organ tune. He couldn't help swaying and wiggling to the music, which was fine because the band was dancing too.

Four songs had gone by before Joe remembered why they'd come in.

"Well," Wilmer was saying, "we'd better pack it up for the night. They use this room for line dancing in the evenings."

"Wait!" Joe cried. "Can we ask you some questions?"

Wilmer shrugged. "Sure," he said.

Frank and Joe told Wilmer and his bandmates why they were there, including everything that had happened at Paul's party and what they knew about the Battle of the Bands. The band members were sympathetic, but they didn't seem to know anything.

"I feel terrible for this young man," Wilmer said, "but I'd never heard of Crush until we got the list of bands playing in the battle. We have a bass guitar in Geezers with Accordions, but it's played by my friend Clyde over there, and he's had it longer than you kids have been alive."

Joe looked over at Clyde, a tall, skinny African American gentleman. "I'd be more than happy to let this young boy borrow it so he can play in the battle," Clyde said. "Just tell him to find me after our set."

Joe nodded. "I'll do that," he said. "But he's pretty attached to Lucy."

Wilmer nodded. "I'm pretty attached to my Lucy too," he said. "Anyhow, we don't much care about winning the Battle of the Bands. We just love to play for an audience. So we thank you, boys."

Joe looked at his brother and smiled.

"Thanks for letting us listen," Frank said.

Joe felt about a million times better than he had on the bus. But as he and Frank headed out to catch another bus home, he knew they were no closer to solving the mystery of what had happened to Lucy than they'd been that morning.

# 7

# Back to the *Ws*

*So as you see,*

*It's you and me.*

*Eternity!*

*Just wait and see.*

Beats pounded all around Frank as a quintet of high school girls stomped toward him and his brother. Then the girls stomped back, wiggled left and right, and spun in a huge circle. The song ended with all the girls doing somersaults at the same time.

"So as you can see," said the lead singer as the music stopped—she isn't even out of breath!—"we don't even use a bass guitar in Babraham Lincoln. We're all about dance music."

Frank was feeling waaaaay out of his comfort zone. "Okay. Thank you very much. Bye," he mumbled, grabbing a gaping Joe and pulling him out of the Bayport High School gym. "Let's head back to the tree house," he told his brother. "We need to think this over."

Friday had arrived, and the boys were no closer to finding out what had happened to Lucy. They'd talked to the four other competing bands now (Judy Mirimoto, the lead singer of the Rock-a-Byes, a folk band made up entirely of moms, had talked with them yesterday), and no one they'd spoken to seemed like a believable thief. Worse still, the Battle was taking place that night. Lucy was still missing. And Dylan was kind of a mess.

"Okay," said Frank, picking up the marker as they looked at what they'd written days ago on the whiteboard. "Let's look at what we have."

Who?
What?—Stole Dylan's bass
When?—During Paul's party
Where?—From Paul's yard
Why?
How?

"It's the Why and How we're stuck on," Frank pointed out. "We thought it was someone from a rival band trying to keep Crush from winning. But we can't find any evidence of that. What if someone stole it for a totally different reason?"

"Like what?" Joe asked.

Frank shrugged. He couldn't come up with another reason—that was the problem. "They don't like Dylan?" he asked. "They hate music?"

Joe frowned. "But it had to be someone at the birthday party," he said, "and they all seemed like huge Crush fans, remember? The minute Dylan and his buddies started setting up, it was all anyone could talk about."

Frank sighed. Joe was right, and he felt totally stumped.

"Joe, I hate to say it," he said, "but I'm not sure we're going to find Lucy in time for the Battle of the Bands."

Joe hung his head. "I was just wondering the same thing."

"I think we'd better call Dylan," Frank said.

Joe reluctantly got to his feet. "I don't *want* to," he said, "but I think you're right. We have to tell Dylan the truth."

Frank put down the marker. Together, the boys slowly climbed down the ladder and ambled across their backyard to the house. They told Aunt Gertrude they needed to make a phone call, then settled down in their father's study to call Dylan.

Frank dialed the number.

*Riiiiing. Riiiing.*

"Wouldn't it be great if Dylan had found it by now?" Joe said. "Like, it was in his closet the whole time and he just forgot to tell us."

Frank gave his brother an *Are you kidding?* look. "That would mean we did all this investigating for nothing," he pointed out.

"Yeah," agreed Joe, looking dreamily out the window, "but it would mean he had Lucy back and they could play at the battle tonight."

As Frank was thinking that over, a voice picked up on the other end of the line. "Hello?"

It was Paul.

"Hi, Paul," Frank said. "It's Frank and Joe Hardy. Listen, is your brother, Dylan, around? We need to talk to him."

There was silence for a moment. "Um . . . gosh . . . Dylan isn't home," Paul said finally.

But before Frank could think of what to say next, someone else picked up. "Hello?"

Frank recognized the voice right away. "Hey, Dylan," he said. "It's Frank and Joe Hardy. We need to talk to you about Lucy."

"Oh, okay." Dylan's voice sounded a little sad at the mention of his beloved guitar. "Want to come over now? I'm not doing anything." He paused. “I don’t have much to do now that I can’t play Lucy.”

Frank met Joe’s eye. *Sad,* Joe mouthed.

“Okay,” said Frank. “We’ll hop on our bikes and be right over.”

“See you soon,” Dylan said, and hung up.

# 8

# Missing Lucy

Joe and Frank looked at each other sadly as Frank rang the doorbell at Paul and Dylan's house.

"It feels like we're giving up," Joe said, shaking his head.

"We're not giving up," Frank said reasonably. "We're just telling Dylan the truth. We can keep looking for Lucy, even after the Battle of the Bands."

But Joe still felt bad. "This may be the first case the Hardy boys couldn't solve."

Frank frowned. "Don't say that. We still might solve it."

The door opened, and both boys looked up to see Dylan at the door—or Dylan as he probably looked right after he got out of bed. His long curls stuck out in every direction, and he was wearing a T-shirt and sweatpants that looked like he might have slept in them. Joe breathed in and winced. *Has Dylan showered today?* It didn't smell like it.

"Hey, guys," Dylan said glumly, and Joe realized that he hadn't brushed his teeth, either. "Sorry I'm kind of a mess. Without Lucy, I've just been watching cartoons all day. You know, trying to forget about the battle tonight."

"Maybe you should shower," Frank said, and Joe winced again. Frank liked to tell it like it was. "You might feel better if you were clean."

Dylan seemed to think about it. "I think I would just be clean and sad," he said. "Anyway, come in, you guys."

He led the boys through the living room—Joe spotted a dent in the couch that looked just about Dylan-size—and into the kitchen. A pitcher of lemonade sat on the table with three glasses and a package of cookies. Dylan plopped onto a chair.

"So you guys wanted to talk about Lucy," he said, hope lighting his eyes. "Did you find her?"

Joe glanced at Frank, clearing his throat. "Um," he said after a moment, deciding to follow Frank's lead and tell it like it was, "no."

Dylan seemed to sink. "Oh," he said. "I figured you probably hadn't. If you had, you would have told me on the phone."

Frank jumped in. "We're really sorry," he said. "We talked to a lot of people and followed a lot of leads. But nobody knew anything."

"We've been looking all week," Joe added. "But . . . I guess we haven't been looking in the right places."

Dylan nodded, but he didn't say anything. Then he put his head in his hands.

Joe was feeling really bad now. He looked at Frank, hoping his brother would know what to say.

"Um . . . we did get you a bass guitar you can use to play tonight, though," Frank told Dylan. "If you want it."

Dylan didn't move. "I dunno," he said quietly. "It won't be Lucy."

"Well, no," Joe agreed, "but it would be a way to make music, right?"

"And maybe help Crush win the Battle of the Bands," Frank pointed out.

Dylan seemed to think that over. "Maybe that wouldn't be so bad," he said slowly. "I really do miss making music. Maybe making music, even without Lucy, would make me feel better."

Joe nodded. "Maybe. It's worth a shot, right?"

Dylan raised his head from the table and sat up. It seemed like he was coming back to life. He sniffed, and then wrinkled his nose. "I stink," he said.

"Kind of," said Frank.

Dylan shook his head. "Well, thanks for trying to find Lucy, you guys. How do I get this bass tonight?"

"Talk to a guy named Clyde who plays with Geezers with Accordions," Joe said. "He'll hook you up."

Dylan thanked them again. "You guys want some lemonade and cookies?" he asked. "I'd better go take a shower before the battle."

"No thanks," said Frank, standing up from the table. "Hey, is Paul around? I'd like to say hi while we're here."

Dylan nodded. "Sure, he's in his room. Follow me."

He led them back through the living room and up a set of stairs to a bright hallway. A closed door was covered with cartoon drawings and a sign that said THIS IS PAUL'S LAIR—KEEP OUT! Joe could hear the sounds of a video game being played inside.

Dylan ignored the sign and knocked on the door. "Hey, Paul!" he yelled. "Paul! Your friends are here, man!"

The bleeps and bloops of the video game stopped, and Joe could hear someone slowly walking to the door. The door opened, and Paul blinked up at them. He looked from Dylan to Frank to Joe. He didn't look very happy to see any of them.

"Hi," said Frank. "We were here to see your brother, so we wanted to say hello."

Paul didn't smile. "Hello," he said.

Joe tried to look past Paul to the TV that was hooked up to a state-of-the-art game console. "Is that Joyride you're playing?" he asked.

Paul nodded. "Yeah," he said, seeming to remember his manners. "Do you guys, uh, want to come in and play?"

"Just for a few minutes," said Frank. "We need to get home in time for Mom and Dad to take us to the Battle of the Bands."

Paul led them inside, and Dylan headed off to take a shower. Paul quickly explained the rules of

Joyride, and he handed a controller to Frank for the boys to share, while he took the other one. He pressed start and the music began playing, and soon Joe was lost in one of his favorite places: the world of video games. Joyride was just as awesome as all the gaming magazines said it was! He had just jumped into a brand-new Mustang and was preparing for a drive down the Malibu coast when suddenly Joe's thumb slipped and he dropped the controller.

"Arrrrgh!" he cried. "Pause it, please, Paul! Hold on!"

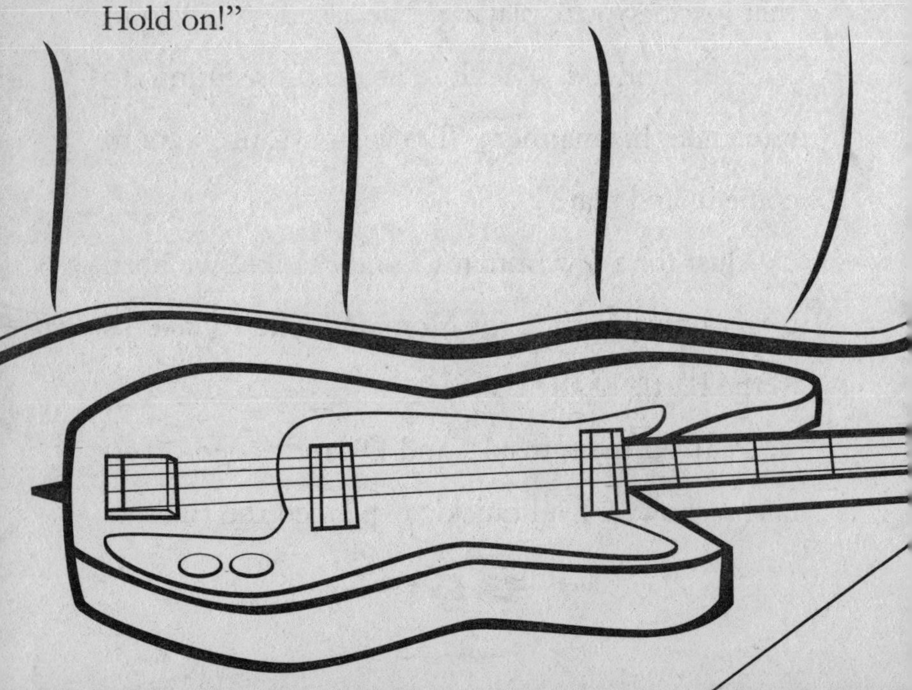

“Wait!” cried Paul, but Joe had already scrambled down to all fours and was peering underneath Paul’s bed.

At first he wasn’t sure what he was looking at. It sure wasn’t the controller. The thing Paul had stashed under his bed was candy-apple red and as shiny as patent leather. Joe’s mouth dropped open as the truth hit him.

*“LUCY!”* he cried, not quite believing it.

# 9

# The Battle Is Won

No sooner had Joe shouted Lucy's name than Frank heard the shower down the hall stop running. There was a series of thumps, then a door opening, and then the door to Paul's room flew open and Dylan stood before them, soaking wet and wearing a terry cloth robe.

"Did somebody say 'Lucy'?" he asked hopefully.

Joe sat up. "Um," he said, looking unsure. "I think . . . I think I found Lucy."

Frank looked at Paul. Paul's mouth was hanging

open, and he looked pale, like he'd just been caught. Frank heard more footsteps, and then Paul's mom appeared at the doorway.

"What's going on here?" she asked.

Dylan pointed to Joe. "This dude thinks he found Lucy," he said.

She tilted her head. "Oh?" she asked.

Joe nodded, then looked at Paul. "Lucy is . . . well . . ."

Paul gulped. "She's under my bed," he admitted.

Paul's mom frowned. "What on earth?" she asked. She walked over to the side of Paul's bed, then crouched down and looked underneath. "Oh my gosh!" she cried, then reached over and pulled out Lucy.

Dylan's face split into a huge smile. "Lucy!" he cried, running over and grabbing her.

Paul's mom was getting to her feet. "Paul," she said, eyeing her son, "is there something you want to tell us?"

Paul didn't look like he wanted to tell anybody anything. In fact, he kind of looked like he'd eaten a bad burrito. But he blinked a few times, looked down at the floor, and finally said, in a very quiet voice, "I stole Lucy."

Dylan, who had been hugging his guitar, gave his brother a startled look. "You did what?"

Paul cleared his throat and said louder, "I stole her, Dylan. I'm sorry. I stole your guitar."

Dylan frowned, and a funny little squiggle appeared on his forehead. "Why would you do that? I was a *mess* without Lucy!"

Paul looked down at the floor again and shrugged. "Well . . . um . . . the truth is, I guess I was kind of jealous."

"Jealous?" Dylan asked, still looking confused. "Of me or Lucy?"

"Both," Paul said with a sigh. "Before you got Lucy and started playing with Crush, you used to hang out with me all the time!" He paused. "Remember?"

Dylan frowned again. "We still do hang out together, bro."

Paul shook his head. "No, we don't," he insisted. "Not as much. And at my birthday party, when everyone stopped paying attention to me the minute you and the band started setting up, I just . . . I dunno . . . I got really *mad.* I tried to forget about it and just play with my friends, but I couldn't. After I got out in musical chairs . . . well . . . nobody was paying attention to me." He paused and looked up at his mom. "Dylan and his friends had gone inside. Lucy was just sitting there alone, and I . . . I went and got her and ran to my room."

Paul's mom looked upset. "Paul, no matter how mad or jealous you were, that's no excuse for stealing Dylan's guitar. You saw how unhappy he was! And he really needed it for the competition!"

Paul sighed. "I know," he said, shrugging. "I knew as soon as I stashed Lucy under my bed that stealing her was a stupid thing to do. And the sadder Dylan got, the worse I felt. But by then I didn't know how to tell everyone the truth." He looked at Frank and Joe. "In a way, I guess it's a good thing you guys came over and caught me."

Dylan shook his head as if he were shaking it all off. "Whatever, little buddy. Look, I'm sorry we haven't been hanging out enough. If you were mad enough to steal Lucy, it must have been bothering you a lot. From now on, you and I are going to do lots more stuff together. In fact, forget the battle tonight. We can stay in and play video games."

Paul grinned. "That's nice of you," he said, "but no. You *have* to play in the battle. After you were so upset all week, I think you *need* to play that guitar."

Dylan chuckled, hugging Lucy close. "Too true," he said. "All right, everyone get ready to rock out!" He strummed a little tune, then pointed at Paul and the boys. "Bayport Battle of the Bands. Be there or be square, kids. Now that I've got Lucy back, I think Crush is going to *crush* the competition!"

Frank and Joe sat with their parents and Aunt Gertrude in the Bayport Auditorium later that night as Susie Zermeño came out onstage.

"Let's have nice round of applause for all the bands who performed tonight!" she said, and the auditorium erupted in applause.

"I think we can all agree that all five bands did Bayport proud," Ms. Zermeño went on.

Joe nodded at his brother. "You can say that again," he said. Each of the five bands competing in the battle had played an amazing set. They had all gotten the crowd to go wild, and Frank's heart was still pounding with excitement. He wasn't sure he'd ever seen so much great live music in one place!

Crush had played "Coo-Coo-Cool My Heart," along with a new song Dylan said he'd just written, called “Requiem for Lucy.” They’d really rocked out, and the crowd went nuts, dancing in their seats. Frank could see why all his classmates were such big Crush fans.

But Geezers with Accordions had been pretty amazing too. They’d had the whole audience grooving, singing along with their songs. Wilmer and his friends had clearly been having the time of their lives, and the audience loved it. When they finished their set, Wilmer had started the audience chanting “Zydeco! Zydeco! Zydeco!”

The Rock-a-Byes had quieted things down with some great folk music, and Babraham Lincoln had gotten the whole audience to their feet with their gymnastic-tastic performance of their original song “Dance Like Your Life Depends on It.” But the real showstopper, amazingly enough, had been the Mean Willies. It turned out Adam’s boasts hadn’t been empty after all: he was an *incredible* drummer. In fact, watching him rock out on the Mean Willies' "I Told You to Stop Talking," Frank thought that maybe Adam had finally found his true calling. He was the best drummer Frank had ever seen, that was for sure.

"But there can be only one winner," Ms. Zermeño said. "So if you'll bear with us for just five minutes, I'm going to go discuss with my fellow judges."

She disappeared off the side of the stage, and recorded music started playing. Joe elbowed his brother. "Who do you think will win?"

Frank shrugged. "I really have no idea. They were all so good!"

"Oh, I agree," said Aunt Gertrude, smoothing her dance-tousled hair. "These bands rival any group I ever saw perform in New York City!"

Just then, Frank saw Dylan approach, still wearing Lucy safely strapped around his shoulder.

"Hey, guys," Dylan greeted the boys. "I really

can't thank you enough for helping me find Lucy."

Frank smiled. "Well, as it turns out, she was right under your nose the whole time!"

Dylan laughed. "Well, one thing's for sure—I'm never letting her out of my sight again!"

As he said that, Paul walked up with two sodas. "Here, bro," he said, handing one to Dylan.

"Thanks, little dude," Dylan said with a smile, raising the cup to his lips. "Thanks for being our roadie tonight," he added after taking a sip. "You're really great with the equipment. We could use your help on all our gigs."

Paul grinned. "Sure. But we need to play one video game for every gig I help out on."

"Deal," said Dylan, shaking his brother's hand. As they let go, Susie Zermeño ran back up onto the stage.

"Okay, okay!" she called. "We've tallied up the votes and we have our winners!"

A hush fell over the crowd. Everyone was eager to hear who'd won the Bayport Battle of the Bands.

"In third place," Susie said, "we have Geezers with Accordions!"

Frank and Joe clapped wildly, and Joe let out an ear-splitting whistle. "Go Wilmer!" he yelled. Wilmer Mack and his bandmates ran up onstage to get their trophy, all beaming from ear to ear. They laughed and waved, and the crowd chanted "Zydeco! Zydeco! Zydeco!" as they ran offstage.

Susie came back to the microphone. "In second place," she said, "we have . . . Crush!"

Dylan let out a whoop, and he and his bandmates ran onstage to get their trophy. Dylan held up Lucy and strummed a couple of notes, and the audience cheered even louder. The band stumbled offstage, and Susie came back to the center.

"And now," she said, "this year's winner of the Bayport Battle of the Bands, winning a cash prize and a weekly gig at Keen Beans, as well as the title of the very best band in Bayport, is . . ."

She paused, and Frank felt his heart thumping. Who would it be?

"The Mean Willies!"

Frank looked at his brother and began applauding loudly. Adam Ackerman had won! And the weird thing was, Frank was really happy for him. He'd totally earned it; he'd learned how to play the drums, practiced hard, and was *really* good at it. *Maybe playing the drums for Adam is like solving mysteries for Joe and me,* Frank thought. *Just something he was meant to do.*

Adam and his buddies got up onstage, Adam pumping his fists like he'd just won the Super Bowl. Frank and his brother clapped and whooped. The audience seemed to love the Mean Willies. The applause was so loud, Frank could barely hear himself think.

After the cheers died down and the Mean Willies

left the stage, Frank turned to Joe. "Let's find Adam and congratulate him," he suggested.

Joe nodded. "It's the least we can do after the way we treated him at lunch the other day," he said.

The boys searched the auditorium and finally found Adam near the stage door, chatting with a bunch of older kids.

"Hey," said Frank, gently touching Adam's shoulder, "congratulations! The Mean Willies really *are* an amazing band."

Adam looked surprised to see the Hardy boys, but he smiled at Frank's words. "Thanks," he said. "We practiced really hard."

"You're a great drummer, Adam," Joe added sincerely.

"Thanks," Adam said, looking pleased. Then one of the older boys jostled him and said, "Ooh, how sweet." Adam frowned.

"I mean," he said, "maybe someday, if you're lucky, you kids will be good at something too. Because you stink at baseball."

The older boy laughed, and Adam turned away, chuckling. Frank looked at Joe and shrugged, smiling.

"Some things never change," he said.

# 10

## Tree House Triumph!

Frank and Joe climbed up to their tree house, and Joe ran over to the whiteboard and grabbed the marker. *Secret Files Case #10,* he wrote, and then, in big letters next to it, *SOLVED!*

"We did it," Joe said happily, reading the words over and over. "You were right, Frank. We found Lucy in the end."

Frank smiled. "Let's fill in all six *W*s, shall we?"

Joe turned back to the board. He read the first *W* out loud: "Who?"

"We know that now," Frank said happily. "The person who stole Dylan's guitar is his brother, Paul."

"Paul," Joe scratched in beside the word "Who." "What, When and Where stay the same," he said, reading what they'd written at the beginning of the case:

Who?—Paul

What?—Stole Dylan's bass

When?—During Paul's party

Where?—From Paul's yard

Why?

How?—Paul grabbed it when Dylan wasn't looking.

The only unanswered word on the whiteboard was "Why." It had been the hardest question, and Joe knew that he and Frank had made a lot of mistakes in trying to answer it.

"Why?" Joe said, lifting the marker.

"Because he wanted Dylan to spend more time with him," Frank answered. "That's why Paul stole Lucy."

Joe wrote that on the whiteboard. With the case solved and all six *W*s filled in, Joe and his brother just looked at the board for a few minutes, feeling proud.

"We learned a lot on this case," Frank said.

Joe nodded. "You can say that again," he agreed. "For one thing, we learned what Speedy's mom tried to tell us, that everyone is innocent until proven guilty."

"Right," Frank agreed. "And that means that unless we're really sure someone has done something—until we have proof—we have to treat everyone with respect."

"Even bullies like Adam Ackerman," Joe added.

"Even when it's hard," Frank agreed.

"I learned something else," Joe said, putting down the marker and looking at his brother. "I learned that sometimes, things aren't as simple as they seem."

Frank's eyes widened. "That's true," he said. "We thought the only reason for someone to steal Dylan's guitar was to keep Crush from performing in the Bayport Battle of the Bands, but that wasn't it at all."

Joe nodded again. "We have to remember that from now on," he said. "Sometimes you need to look a little harder to find the right answer!"

Before Frank could reply, the boys were interrupted by a sharp *beep*: Frank's watch alarm.

"It's three o'clock!" Frank said in an excited voice. "Time to head to Golden Lanes!"

Joe and his brother were going to see their friend Wilmer Mack at his apartment building—but not just for a casual visit. Clyde was teaching Joe to play the bass guitar, and Wilmer was teaching Frank to play the accordion. Neither boy had made anything that could really be called music yet, but they sure had made a lot of noise. And they sure were having a lot of fun!

"Now that Dylan has Lucy back and he and Paul are cool again, I'm glad we worked on this case," Joe told Frank as they walked to the garage to get their bikes.

"Why's that?" asked Frank.

"Before this case, I only listened to music on my iPod," Joe said, settling on his bike and pedaling down the driveway. "Who knew that making music was this much fun!"

## SECRET FILES CASE #10: SOLVED!

Hey, I have a great idea—the three of us should start a ROCK BAND!
Great idea!
Let's do it!

BAYPORT
Hey, what are you guys doing?
Choosing instruments. We're starting a band!

BAYPORT
Hey, can I join your band?
Sure!
Great! Before we choose instruments, I have an idea. . . .

Before we figure out what to play, we need a funky look!
I like this.
This is awesome!
HATS

BAYPOR
Hey! Why don't we come up with a logo we can print on the drums!

I don't know. . . .
Edgier!
More dragons!

Perfect!

BAYPORT
Wait—we need a name for our band!

How about the Babylonian Fire-Breathers?
No, no! We should be Fire-Breathing Ninja!

HOURS LATER . . .
Okay. The Fire-Breathing Frogs of Fury it is!

BAYPORT
IC
CLOSED
Oh no!

MUSIC
I know! Let's go back to our house— we can find stuff to use as instruments!
Awesome!

Perfect!
Cool!

A one, two, three, four!

Hmmmm.
VIDEO ROCK STAR GAME
Who wants to play video games instead?

Available on the
App Store

HeR
INTERACTIVE